To Phoebe,

Big Bill and the Lark...g Lambs

Written by Jayne Baldwin

Illustrated by Shalla Gray

Happy
Reading

Jayne
Baldwin.

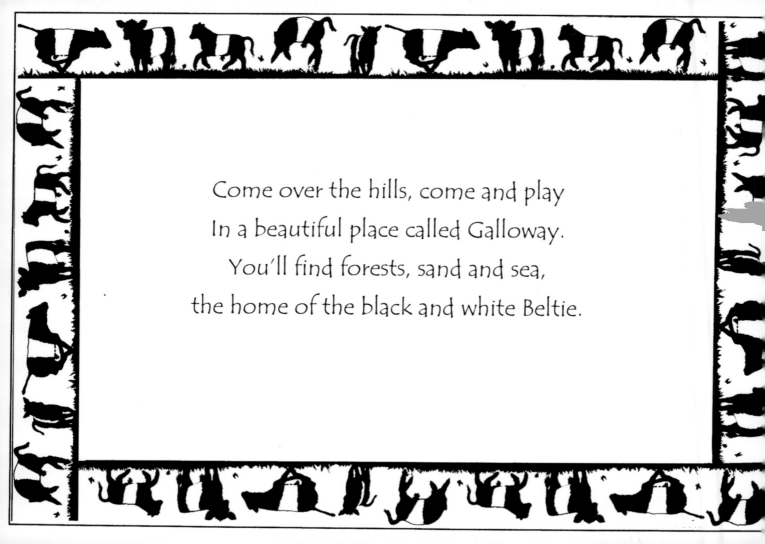

Come over the hills, come and play
In a beautiful place called Galloway.
You'll find forests, sand and sea,
the home of the black and white Beltie.

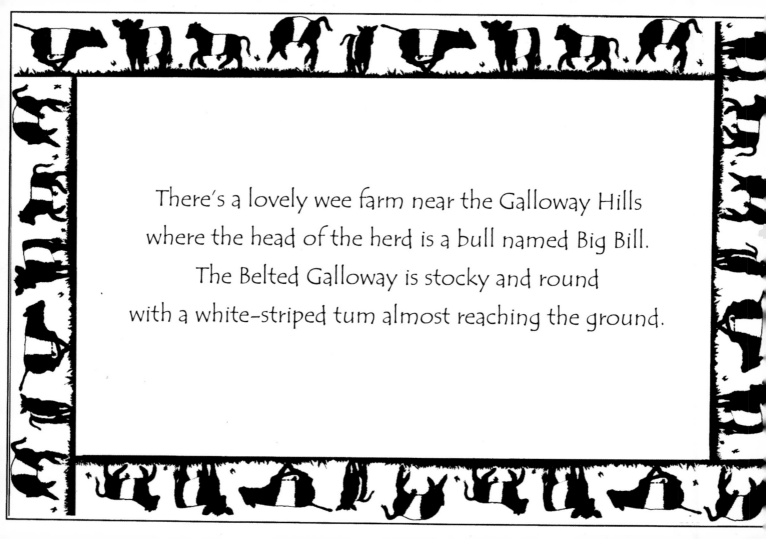

There's a lovely wee farm near the Galloway Hills
where the head of the herd is a bull named Big Bill.
The Belted Galloway is stocky and round
with a white-striped tum almost reaching the ground.

It was a dull, dreich day at Benyellary Farm,
Farmer Bob found some work in the warmth of the barn.
Outside in the field Bertie and Buntie were bored;
they yawned as they heard their mum softly snore.

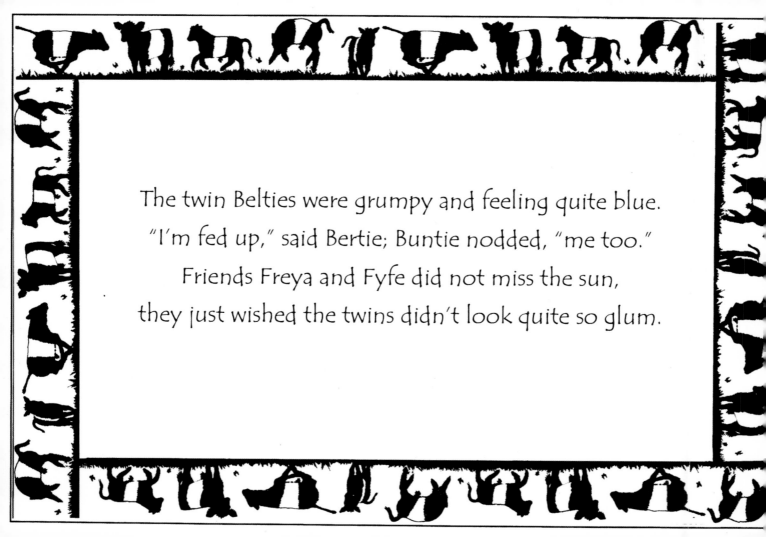

The twin Belties were grumpy and feeling quite blue.
"I'm fed up," said Bertie; Buntie nodded, "me too."
Friends Freya and Fyfe did not miss the sun,
they just wished the twins didn't look quite so glum.

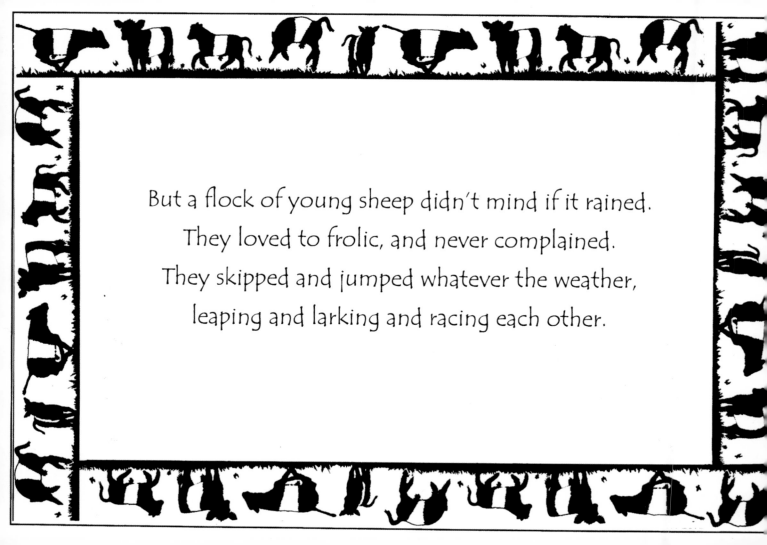

But a flock of young sheep didn't mind if it rained.
They loved to frolic, and never complained.
They skipped and jumped whatever the weather,
leaping and larking and racing each other.

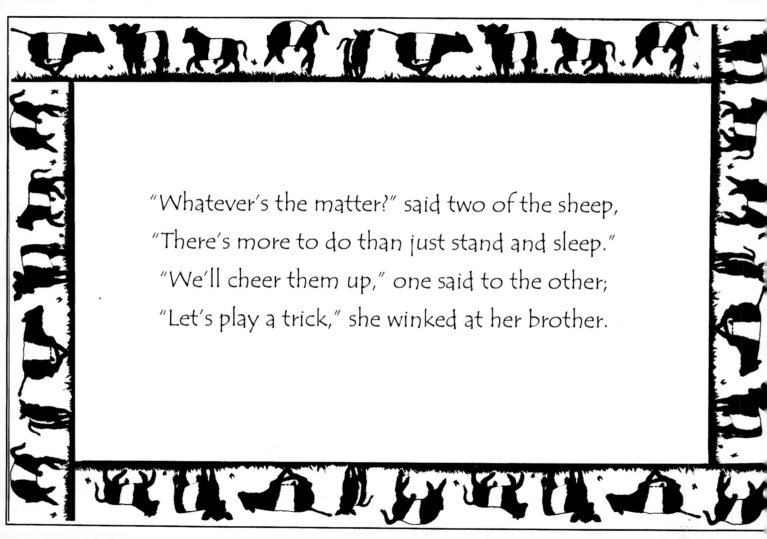

"Whatever's the matter?" said two of the sheep,
"There's more to do than just stand and sleep."
"We'll cheer them up," one said to the other;
"Let's play a trick," she winked at her brother.

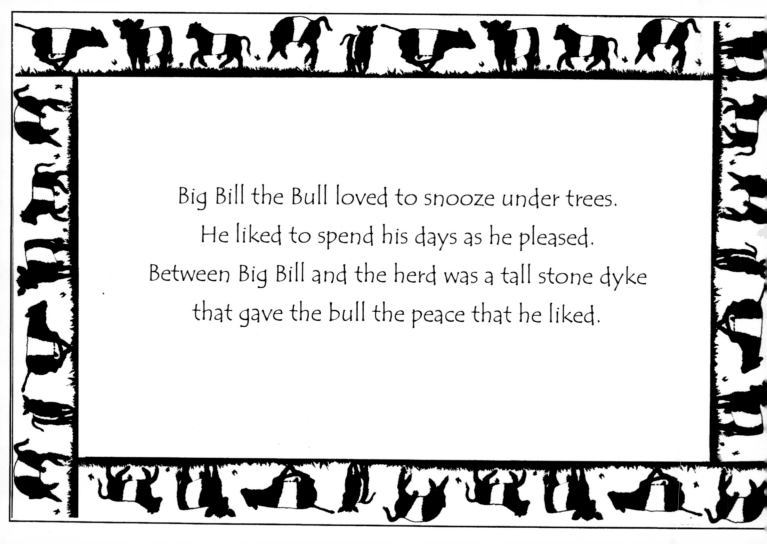

Big Bill the Bull loved to snooze under trees.
He liked to spend his days as he pleased.
Between Big Bill and the herd was a tall stone dyke
that gave the bull the peace that he liked.

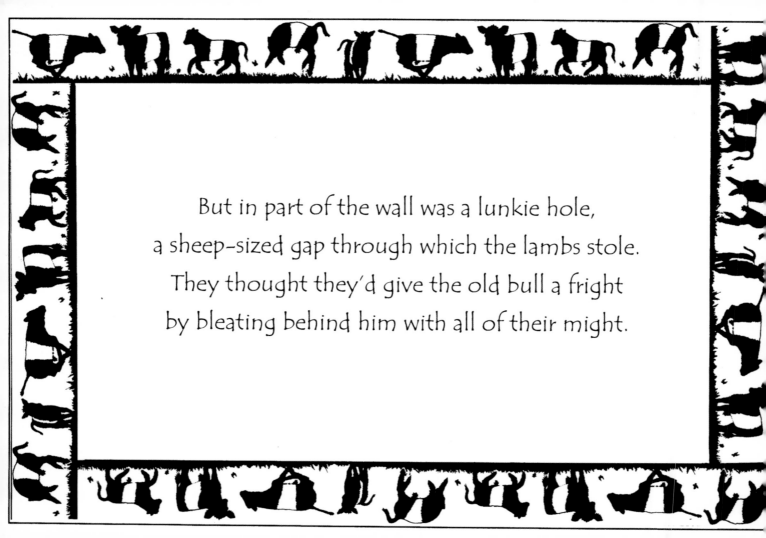

But in part of the wall was a lunkie hole,
a sheep-sized gap through which the lambs stole.
They thought they'd give the old bull a fright
by bleating behind him with all of their might.

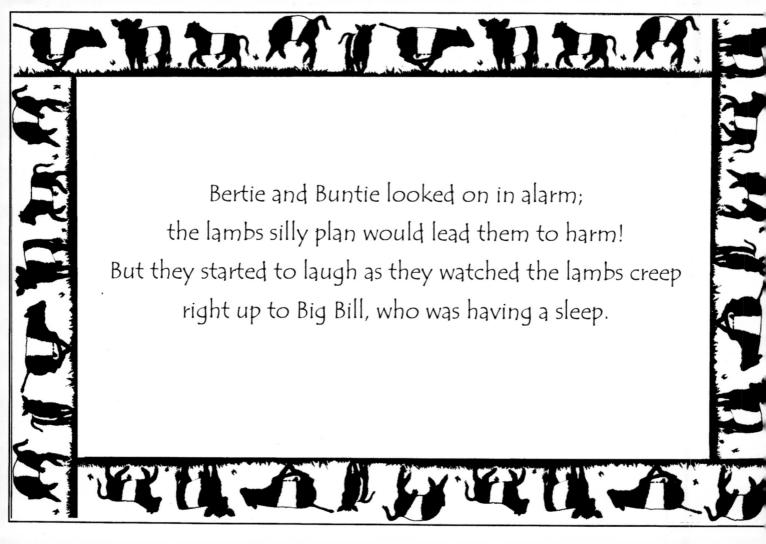

Bertie and Buntie looked on in alarm;
the lambs silly plan would lead them to harm!
But they started to laugh as they watched the lambs creep
right up to Big Bill, who was having a sleep.

He was quietly snoozing, as sound as a log,
but the lambs' loud bleats made him jump like a frog!
He'd been dreaming of winning a big silver cup,
but now he was angry; he'd been woken up!

Bill looked around for the source of the shock,
and saw the wee sheep who'd escaped from the flock.
They stood there shaking their tails all a-wiggle
and from over the wall he could hear the twins giggle.

Big Bill was angry to hear such a sound,
and with his big hoof he pawed at the ground.
He turned on the lambs, who saw the bull snort,
they knew this wasn't the time to cavort.

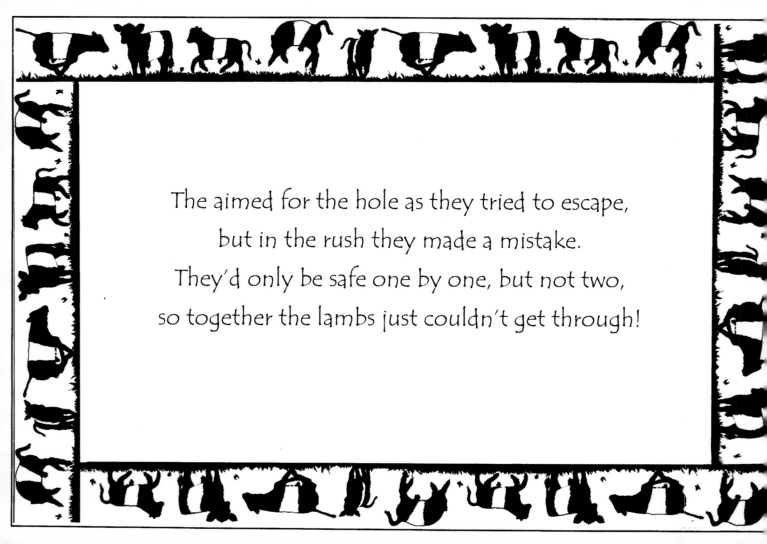

The aimed for the hole as they tried to escape,
but in the rush they made a mistake.
They'd only be safe one by one, but not two,
so together the lambs just couldn't get through!

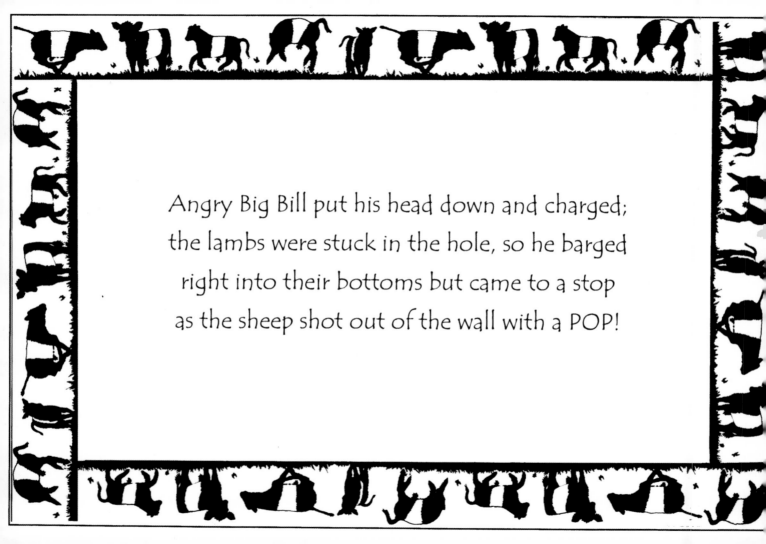

Angry Big Bill put his head down and charged;
the lambs were stuck in the hole, so he barged
right into their bottoms but came to a stop
as the sheep shot out of the wall with a POP!

The lambs went tumbling head over heels,
rolling along like a tractor's big wheels;
eventually landing up in a heap
of tangled and dizzy, silly wee sheep!

Bertie laughed, "I'm glad it's not sunny,
I've never seen anything quite this funny!"
And Big Bill the Bull wandered back to his wood,
hoping his charge would stop tricksters for good.

More adventures with Big Bill:

Big Bill the Beltie Bull

Written & illustrated by Shalla Gray

Big Bill's Beltie Bairns

written by Jayne Baldwin   illustrated by Shalla Gray

Jayne Baldwin
&
Shalla Gray

Curlytale Books

www.curlytalebooks.co.uk

More Titles From Curly Tale Books:

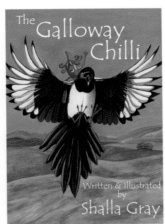

www.curlytalebooks.co.uk

ISBN 978-0-9576402-7-6
Published by Curly Tale Books Ltd
34 Main Street
Kirkcowan DG8 0HG
www.curlytalebooks.co.uk

Design & Layout by Shalla Gray
Printed by J&B Print, 32A Albert Street,
Newton Stewart, DG8 6EJ

About the Author and Illustrator

You would never believe it from this picture, but Jayne & Shalla have seven children between them. Don't they wear it well!
Artistic licence aside, together Jayne & Shalla run Curly Tale Books, an independent publishing company based in Wigtown, Scotland's National Booktown.
Big Bill and the Larking Lambs is their ninth publication.
And yes, Shalla does own a three-legged dog.